# The Goosehill Gang
## and the
## Test Paper Thief

by Mary Blount Christian
illustrated by Betty Wind

Do not set yourself against the man who wrongs
you. If someone slaps you on the right cheek,
turn and offer him your left.
Matthew 5:39 NEB

Publishing House
St. Louis

To Beth Carrington,
Valley Oaks Elementary,
for her friendship and devotion.

Concordia Publishing House, St. Louis, Missouri
Copyright © 1976 Concordia Publishing House
Manufactured in the United States of America

Library of Congress Cataloging in Publication Data

Christian, Mary Blount.
    The Goosehill Gang and the test paper thief.

        SUMMARY: Tubby is unjustly accused of stealing the answers to a test at school. He knows who really did it and doesn't want to tell.
        [1. School stories] I. Title.
PZ7.C4528Gq          [E]          76-3639
ISBN 0-570-03608-9

"Last one to the playground is a rotten egg!" Beth called to the other members of the Goosehill Gang.

Pete and Don raced ahead of her. Tubby arrived last. His face was pink, and he was puffing hard. "Oh, rats!" he said between puffs. "I forgot my lunch. It's on my desk. I'll be right back."

Tubby hurried into the school building. He had almost turned into the classroom when he stopped short. Someone was in there.

Tubby ducked behind the opened door. He peered through the crack. It was Lester, the school bully. He was pawing through some papers on the teacher's desk.

4

Tubby watched as Lester crammed one of the
papers into his pocket and crushed the others into the
desk.

"That creepy Lester!" Tubby said to himself. He wanted to go in and get his lunch. But he hated to face Lester. "Rubba dubba Tubby!" Lester would shout at him every time. He was always punching Tubby on the arm, or shoving him out of lines. Lester knew that Tubby wouldn't fight back.

Tubby walked back to the playground. "Where's your lunch?" Beth asked.

"I . . . I guess I forgot to bring it," he said.

Pete shoved half of his sandwich toward Tubby. "Here," he said.

"No, thanks!" Tubby said.

"Gosh, Tubby's not eating?" Beth teased. "He must be getting sick!"

Pete frowned. "You may be right, Beth. Tubby is as pale as an old sheet. And he's shaking too."

"I'm just not hungry," Tubby said. "That's all, honest."

"Sure, Tub," Beth said. "We were just teasing you."

Later in class everyone sat at their desks. Tubby looked around at Lester. He wondered what he'd been doing at Mrs. Smith's desk at lunch.

Mrs. Smith opened one desk drawer, then another. She sorted papers and turned them over. She looked through everything inside and outside her desk.

Finally Mrs. Smith said, "I want all of you to empty your desk right now, while I am watching."

Noisily the children pulled papers and books and assorted pencils from their desks.

Tubby pulled out his lunch sack and papers. He stared at one of the papers on his desk. "Oh, no!" he gasped.

Mrs. Smith walked over. She tapped the paper with her finger and looked at him steadily. "I'm surprised at you, Michael," she said. She was the only one except his mother who called him Michael.

"I . . . I," Tubby mumbled.

"You realize I will have to give you a zero on the math test," Mrs. Smith continued. "I don't see why you would take the answers from my desk. You make good grades, Michael. You don't have to cheat."

The word cheat cut into Tubby like a knife. "I...I didn't take them," he said.

"Then how did the answer sheet get into your desk?"

"I...I can't tell you," he said. Tubby felt hot all over. He could feel Beth's eyes looking at him.

"I want to believe that," Mrs. Smith said. "But it looks very bad." She picked up the paper and returned to her desk.

Tubby felt empty and sick all day. After school he walked slowly from the room. Suddenly he felt a hard shove. "Rubba dubba Tubby is a test thief!" Lester called.

Tubby flushed bright red. He couldn't remember feeling this bad in all his life. Beth waited for him at the bus stop. "Didn't you have time to study?" she asked.

Tubby's jaw stiffened. "So you think I did it too!"

Beth looked down at her feet. "Well, gosh, Tubby.

You said you had to get your lunch. But you came back without it. And it was there in your desk all the time."

"Well, I didn't!" Tubby yelled. "It was... it was..."

"Was what?" Beth asked. "Do you know who took the answers?"

"Yeah," Tubby said. "At least I think I know."

"Well, for gosh sakes. Go tell Mrs. Smith, then," Beth scolded him.

Tubby kicked a rock. "I can't. I just can't."

Pete and Don came up. "We heard what happened, Tubby. You're too smart to pull that!" Don said.

"You too?" Tubby shouted. "Doesn't anybody believe me?"

The gang boarded the bus. They rode silently, unhappily. At last Beth spoke. "I hope you have a good reason for not tattling. Still friends?"

Tubby grinned at her. "Still friends! I hope I have a good reason too."

Tubby scratched his forehead. "I saw someone take that paper, I think. I just wish I had the nerve to face him with it."

Beth's face lit up. "We'll go with you! The Goosehill Gang will help!"

But Tubby shook his head. "This is my mess. I have to work it out myself."

They got off the bus. "Would you tell my mom that I'll be late?" Tubby asked Don. "I guess it is now or never at all."

Tubby stalked off down the street. His fists were clenched so tight they ached.

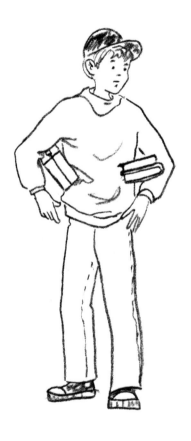

He was on Lester's front porch and about to knock. He heard voices inside. "You ain't got the brains you wuz born with!" a man's voice was yelling.

"But, Paw!" a whiny voice said. Tubby recognized Lester's voice.

"Hush!" the man said. "Look at this flashlight! It's in a million pieces. It is useless now. You ruined it!"

"I just wanted to learn what makes it work, Paw," Lester whimpered.

"Learn! Learn? Of all the stupid . . . ." The voice trailed off. A door slammed somewhere inside. Tubby could hear Lester sobbing.

Quietly Tubby left the porch. He sat on the curb to think. In a while Lester came outside.

His shoulders were slumped. When he saw Tubby, Lester pulled himself straight. "Well! Old rubba dubba Tubby!" Lester teased. "What are you doing around here? Come to beat me up?"

Tubby could see that his eyes were still red and swollen. He stared at Lester, trying to think of just what he should do. Now that he had heard Lester's father it was easy to see why Lester thought being a bully was the only way.

20

Tubby stood to face Lester. His jaw was set tight.
"I came over here to punch you in the nose. But now I
think that I would rather help you to learn your
schoolwork. Then you wouldn't have to cheat."

Lester's mouth flew open. "You knew? You knew
that I took the test paper? You didn't tell! Why?"

Tubby nodded. "I knew. I guess at first I didn't tell because I was scared of you. But now? Well, I guess I just feel I ought to help you because you need a friend."

Lester looked like he was going to cry again. "Wh...why?" He stammered. "I don't understand you."

Tubby shrugged. "I don't quite understand myself. But I guess it has something to do with turning the other cheek when you've been slapped."

Lester shook his head, puzzled. "All that'd get me around here is *two* slapped cheeks," he said sadly. "Did you tell the teacher?" he asked suddenly. "My paw is going to skin me!"

"No," Tubby said. "I didn't tell. Now go get your math book, and I will help you."

The boys worked on math all that afternoon. Tubby was humming when he went to school the next day. He couldn't figure exactly why he was that happy. After all, he told himself, he still had a zero in math.

Tubby had no sooner entered the room when Mrs. Smith called him to her desk. "Michael," she said, "Lester has told me everything. I am restoring your good grade."

Tubby looked around at Lester. He sat in his chair looking small and frightened. He didn't look at all like the bully he was yesterday.

28

Tubby grinned. "Mrs. Smith, will you give the test to Lester again?"

Mrs. Smith raised her eyebrows. "Whatever for?" she asked.

Tubby winked at Lester. "I feel pretty sure that he can pass the test on his own now."

Mrs. Smith agreed. During lunch, Lester took the test. Tubby and the rest of the Goosehill Gang waited outside. Lester came out with a wide grin. "Won't Paw be proud of me?" he said.

"I don't know about that!" Beth said. "But we sure are!"

Suddenly Lester gave Tubby a big shove. "Come on, rubba dubba Tubby!" he shouted.

"Hey!" Tubby yelled. "I thought we were going to be friends!"

Lester shrugged. "Old habits, I guess."

Tubby sighed helplessly. "I have a feeling I'm going to run out of cheeks to turn before this year is over."

Beth giggled. "Come on. Last one to the playground is a rotten egg."

She, Tubby, Pete, and Don raced out into the sunshine.